MW00694839

First published in the United States, Great Britain, Australia, and New Zealand in 1994 by North-South Books, an imprint of Nord-Süd Verlag.

First published in Switzerland under the title Ich wünscht' ich wär . . . ein Vogel. by Michael Neugebauer Verlag AG, Gossau Zurich.

Distributed in the United States by North-South Books, Inc., New York.

Library of Congress Cataloging-in-Publication Data is available
A CIP catalogue record for this book is available from The British Library
ISBN 1-55858-316-5 (trade edition) 10 9 8 7 6 5 4 3 2 1
ISBN 1-55858-317-3 (library edition) 10 9 8 7 6 5 4 3 2 1

Printed in Belgium

A Michael Neugebauer Book

NORTH-SOUTH BOOKS / NEW YORK / LONDON

I Wish I Were...
a Bird

By Eve Tharlet

Mother, I wish I were a bird!

Not a small bird . . . not a tall bird . . .

a just-right bird that loves to fly!

I'd fly with ease
over houses and trees.

1

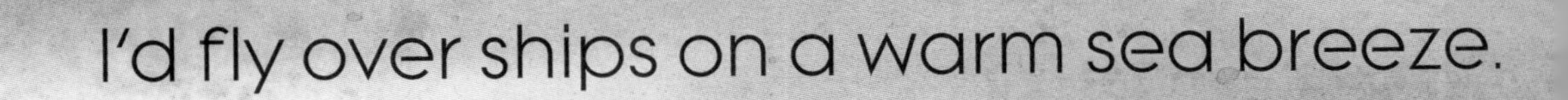

I'd fly over ships on a warm sea breeze.

BIRD

I'd rise and I'd rise to the top of the sky—
Up in the clouds where the big planes fly.

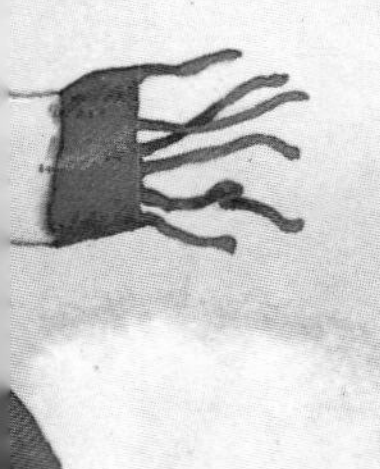

I'd take a short rest
once I got to the moon,

Then fly home for lunch
the next day by noon.

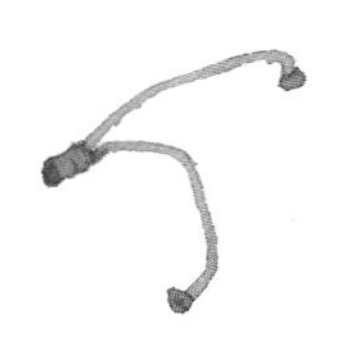

I'd eat every cherry
right off our big tree,

And if you objected,
I'd say, "Tweedle-dee!"

But think about the winter cold.

What would you eat?

And think how wet
you would be when it rains.

And when the stormy winds blow,
little birds can't even fly.

You're right, Mother.

Sooo...

I'll be a bird only on **nice** days!